The Messiah of the Metro Café

a novel by

Ronda Chervin

En Route Books and Media, LLC

Saint Louis, MO

✺ENROUTE
Make the time

En Route Books and Media, LLC
5705 Rhodes Avenue, St. Louis, MO 63109

Copyright © 2022 Ronda Chervin
Cover credit: Sebastian Mahfood using a photo of
the author's grandson, Nicholas Conley

ISBN-13: 979-8-88870-018-1
Library of Congress Control Number: 2022952154

All rights reserved. No part of this booklet may be reproduced, stored in a retrieval system, or transmitted in any form, or by any means, electronic, mechanical, photocopying, or otherwise, without the prior written permission of the author. Queries to chervinronda@gmail.com or 860-759-4521.

1

It was 9:00 A.M., October 24, 2022. The reporters of *The Catholic Weekly of Los Angeles* met in the chief editor's office for their special assignments.

"The old parish church in Santa Monica was burned down by a gang last Wednesday night."

"You got it, Jim," the editor belted out when one of the reporters waved his hand.

"Pope Francis' address to the Ukrainian refugees in Rome."

"Go for it, Melissa."

"This cult leader is influencing some St. Mark's seminarians from his throne in a nearby café."

"I'll take that one," Teresa grinned enthusiastically, catching Jim glancing in her direction.

A few evenings later found Teresa Domingo on a long drive from *The Catholic Weekly*'s office in midtown Los Angeles. She headed north on the Pacific Coast Highway to the Metro Café in Santos near the seminary.

As soon as she was out of the heaviest traffic past Santa Monica, the fifty-year-old brunette reporter, dressed in a fluffy white blouse over blue pants, texted her husband to remind him, "Heat up the dinner I put in the fridge." As per a custom of twenty-five years of marriage, she always ended any call or e-mail or text with the words, "I love you, John."

A half-an-hour before reaching the café, Teresa turned off the news program she always listened to after work. She reviewed what she had learned from the rector of St. Mark's Seminary about this supposed cult leader.

Here is, more or less, what she remembered Fr. Victor O'Brien relating:

"One of our seminarians, Paul Quinn, told me that a group of them had been going every Thursday evening for about a month to this nearby café.

"When he said that, I quipped, 'Probably you're trying to get around being observed at the house 24/7!' He just shook his head.

"Teresa, you may not know that some time ago we forbade the seminarians to go to any place in the evening where alcohol is served. You can guess the reason."

The rector had continued his briefing. "Paul told me that they sit around a table at the Café Metro presided over by a strange hippie-looking guy...who actually looks like Jesus as portrayed in *The Passion* by Jim Caviezel. This man, a kind of New Age Jew, goes by the name of Michael Kaufman."

Reflecting on this, having never seen the movie, Teresa pulled to the side of the road and found a photo of Jim Caviezel in *The Passion*.

Going back to Fr. O'Brien's call, she recalled that the rector had asked Paul Quinn, "What was your first impression of him?"

"I liked what he said at first... you know, all about inner peace... the usual stuff...but then after a few Thursdays I thought that while we might be trying to evangelize him, he might wind up leading some of us astray...if only by providing them excuses for other evening excursions with the cover up that they went to evangelize him in his cabin on the beach."

"Now, Teresa, since you have covered other stories about the seminary, you certainly know that we have to be very careful about these men who will probably be priests...on the other hand, we also don't want to make them feel that we are like detectives watching them all the time...so, as a way of vetting the matter of this supposed new age, cult-like leader, I thought of asking your editor if he might assign you to come and interview him at that Metro Café. The pretext for interviewing him could be that you're writing an article about how Catholics are dialoguing with New Agers."

Thinking about the assignment and the rector's undercover plan, Teresa decided to ask her editor if she could devote several sessions at the café to the research…with time off from her regular work at the paper in recompense. He readily agreed since Teresa was so cooperative when it came to substituting for any reporter who couldn't complete some assignment.

2

At 7:00 PM, Teresa had arrived at the Metro Café in the beach town of Santos. It was just like all the others in the chain, white cement with pictures of subway trains on the front. There were about ten vehicles in the parking lot all the way from sleek convertibles to battered old jeeps.

Teresa thought that maybe since the beach here attracts so many people, and most of them love metro coffee shops, they wouldn't care how out of place pictures of subway trains are at the beach in California.

She grabbed her tote bag out of the seat, quickly checking for the needed items: wallet, cell phone, and a paper notepad, just to give her the look of a reporter of old that most people seemed to like.

Sure enough, in a corner of the café was a table with six seminarians wearing their black pants and white shirts. In the center of the circle was this Michael Kaufman, so different from these others because his face absolutely did look like Jim Caviezel's in *The Passion*.

"Hello, Jesus!" Teresa greeted him, extending her hand.

The seminarians all laughed, but Michael, instead, looked at Teresa with a penetrating stare. He had been told that a Catholic newspaper reporter was writing an article and wanted to interview him. But the stare was more as if he was discerning what spiritual help she personally might need from him.

Teresa put a little note down in shorthand – Messiah complex of New Age gurus: I don't need any help, only you!

Teresa sat down opposite to Michael, and seeing he had nothing in front of him, she waved to the barista to put in her order: "Two cappuccinos, and two bagels with cream cheese, please."

The barista taking the order was 6'6", a slim person in men's clothing but with bright red lipstick, long hair in a high ponytail, a ring on his nose, and fake pearl bracelets on his wrists. If it wasn't for his absolutely flat chest and his male voice, anyone would have been sure this person was a female.

Teresa hadn't seen many non-binaries. She suddenly recalled how horrified she was when, at the beginning of the peace movement, a father whose son had evaded the draft found that the boy had started wearing long hair. This seemed to be the last straw leading the father to kill his son! After long-hair on males became rather popular, this tragedy seemed ever more outlandish. "I don't need to decide about this issue pre-ma-turely," she thought.

Michael, wearing a frayed red plaid shirt on his medium-sized frame, reached across the table to take Teresa's hand. "You are Teresa Domingo, *The Catholic Weekly* reporter who has honored me with an interview. Shall we say a prayer for this encounter to be blessed?"

"Certainly, Michael. Please intone a prayer yourself."

Michael closed his eyes and lifted his hands: "May the Spirit who transcends all divisions flood our gathering with peace."

Teresa speedily wrote down the prayer in shorthand on her notepad.

"Michael, you probably know that in the last decades the Catholic Church has decided that it is better for those of different religions to enter into dialogue with each other instead of perpetuating ignorance, bigotry and even persecution."

Leaning forward, with hands folded in prayer, Michael replied: "As a person with a Jewish background, I am sure that such a circle of friends as ours here would have been unlikely in centuries past."

"I would love to hear more on your background, Michael."

After the barista came with her order, and seconds for all the others, Teresa asked: "So, tell me, were you born here in Southern California?"

"Yes. I was born in 1992. My parents were of Jewish origin but never went to religious services. Even their grandparents didn't celebrate Jewish holidays."

"What was their work?"

"They met at an insurance company. But this company dissolved and after various part-time jobs, for various reasons that I don't want to see in the article you write, they wound up in the tent homeless village near this very beach where I now work as a combination lifeguard and caretaker."

"Fascinating!" Even though Teresa was sure the seminarian friends of Michael knew this back story, they seemed glad to hear it again, so different was this man's background from their own – Catholic middle-class.

"But you went to public school, didn't you?"

"Yes. The few kids of the Tent City went on the bus to school."

"Did you feel accepted by the other children?"

"No. The other boys bullied us, calling us street kids because of our ragged clothing and calling our parents druggies."

"Didn't that make you afraid of going to school?"

"I guess so, but things began to change in Junior High. There was a teacher who was into a self-help group called Recovery International. It was founded by a Jewish psychiatrist in the 1940's before the Twelve-Step program took that name. Abraham Low gradually worked out a whole system for people with problems of anger, anxiety and depression. By changing their daily thoughts, he found, they could change their emotions."

"That's a bit abstract, Michael. Give me an example."

Dark brown eyes, now gleaming with enthusiasm, Michael spoke on. "Here's a simple example: when something upsetting but not dangerous happens, such as leaving your cell phone at home by mistake, instead of screaming and yelling and feeling helpless, you use a Recovery International tool such as saying, 'It's not a 911.'"

Paul Quinn broke in: "It actually works, Ms. Domingo. Michael got us to try it for a week...refusing to get angry over every problem, saying 'it's not a 911' and then trying to find a solution."

"So, back to your being bullied as a street kid by the others at school, the teacher got you to accept the challenge as bad but not a 911 and then do something to solve it?"

"Right on. When the kids called me bad names, I would surprise them by, instead of running away, confronting them, and saying something like – 'I don't know why you don't like me since I like you.'"

"Very interesting, Michael. I'll be back in a minute," Teresa said taking her cellphone with her to the bathroom.

"John, this is turning out very well, so don't wait up. Another hour, at least, before it's over…I love you, John."

Back at the table, Teresa asked: "So, how was High School for you, Michael?"

"Different! I happened to like long hair, but when it grew long enough the other students started calling me Jesus. I would just laugh, but eventually I decided to look Jesus up on the web."

A seminarian who had not yet spoken, piped in: "So, what did you think of our Lord and Messiah, Michael?"

"I was impressed, but when I mentioned him to my parents, they quickly told me that Christians were enemies of the Jews, had persecuted us unmercifully, peaking with Hitler's extermination camps. So, I should not even look into Christianity."

"Some other time, Michael," Teresa said in a matter-of-fact way to avoid looking as if she was evangelizing him, "let me tell you about such groups as Jews for Jesus, Messianic Jews, and the Association of Hebrew-Catholics. Did you go to college?"

"No. I really didn't like school at all. Just when I was about to graduate from High School, my mother got a large inheritance from her father. My parents decided to leave Tent-City and move to Los Angeles. By that time, I had become a real beachcomber since the Tent-City was right on the beach. I didn't want to go with them to the city. I took this job at the beach picking up litter and then moved up to becoming a life-guard as well. I've been doing that ever since."

"Do they pay well?"

"Not really, but I get the use of a cabin on the beach and about $700 a month to buy food."

"And, of course, coffee?"

Michael leaned forward and whispered, "Actually, Teresa…can

I call you Teresa since you are so friendly?"

When Teresa nodded, he confided: "They give me coffee and bagels and donuts for free here because I attract customers – kind of local color. I come every evening after dark. A guy from Tent-City monitors the beach at night for me."

"I know it's off the subject, but just out of curiosity, can I ask if you have lots of girlfriends?"

The seminarians, who would soon make a vow to life-long celibacy, didn't like to bring up this subject with other young men, but they seemed to perk up their ears to hear how Michael would reply.

"I like the beauty in the feminine," he said softly, eyes more dreamy than his usual penetrating spiritual look.

"On the other hand, and maybe some of you seminarians will understand, I find the way most women talk very boring."

A few of the seminarians snickered.

Teresa looked down at her notepad.

"Oh, Ms. Domingo, Teresa..."
Michael grabbed her hand. "I hope
I didn't offend you. I don't mean
intellectual women such as reporters like you."

"Ha! Ha! I know what you
mean, Michael. I find many
women boring also. That's one
reason why I took a job at the
Catholic paper, where most of the
staff are male, even when my children were small."

One of the seminarians had a
question: "Michael, if it isn't too
personal, not for the article for *The*

Catholic Weekly, but just for us, were you sexually active?"

"I never had a steady lover, but I did have casual sex. To avoid becoming a father, I used condoms."

Teresa glanced at the large clock on the wall. "It's almost 9:30 PM, guys. I have so much more I want to ask you. Can I come back next Thursday evening?"

3

The following Thursday, on November 3, after everyone had placed their orders with the dramatic looking barista, Teresa opened this way: "Since I understand this group of seminarians likes to dialogue with you, Michael, could you give me a short mini-lecture about your ideas?"

"As a matter of fact, I made up a sheet of my truths." He took out a little stapled booklet. She could see that these sentences were typed in 20 font.

"Perhaps there is a printer in the office of this café, and they would copy it for me."

Michael stood up and went into the back office, returning in five minutes with a copy of the page.

Speed reading, Teresa smiled. "Wonderful, but suppose you read each one aloud and tell us more about it so we all can benefit."

"Aha, I get to be like a college professor!" Michael smiled. In a voice louder than usual, he began with the first nugget on the list:

"Be the eye in a storm!"

"Because of my job at the beach, I see the progress of many a storm. It took me a while to appreciate the phrase 'the eye of the storm.'

"I realized that while most of the time the stormy rain engulfs the whole ocean and beach area, sometimes, after the last swimmer has fled and I am alone watching from my cabin, that refuge would be a kind of eye in the storm.

"Now, in daily life there is hardly a day without some people going into a kind of storm-like angry conflict."

"You mean, even at our beautiful Southern California beach?" Teresa asked sarcastically.

Michael ignored the comment, eager to return to his insight. "I came to see that, not always, but sometimes, just walking over to the people arguing with each other loudly or even raising fists, my presence could calm them.

"Aha, you mean you can be the eye in the storm."

"Exactly. Not by a warning that if their conflict became worse I would call the police, but rather simply by peacefully saying something like – 'Hope you all are having a nice day at the beach. Nothing's wrong, is there? Their storm would abate."

Paul Quinn made them all laugh by interrupting, "You know, Michael, maybe they should hire you at the seminary!"

Another seminarian added, "And Jesus taught 'Blessed are the peacemakers.'"

Teresa had an impulse to interrupt the semi-lecture format and ask the seminarians what they liked about Michael. One explained:

"He notices everything that happens here, and then talks about it to the strangers…like the way Jesus used examples from life right around him."

Just then, out of the corner of his eye, Michael noticed a young Filipino couple on a bench near their table. The woman dropped a bagel and some of the cream cheese escaped onto the floor. She picked it up and looked at it sadly, as if considering whether she had to throw it out. The young man grabbed it and ate a bite himself.

Michael, loud enough for them to hear, called out "True love, indeed."

The couple laughed. They came over to his table on the way out, and he engaged them in further conversation.

And what do you know? A few weeks later when Teresa came for a third follow up interview, that couple was sitting at a table near him…part of his group!

When the Filipino couple left the café during the interview, one of the seminarians mentioned how in the Philippines some fanatics on

Good Friday volunteer to be cruci-
fied!

"Really?" Michael questioned,
obviously incredulous.

"Of course, only for about ten
minutes, or so," remarked a Filipino seminarian who was sitting at
the table.

Teresa supposed that he didn't
want Michael to think that Catholics were crazy.

Teresa, who had heard about
this strange custom before, was
quick to add: "It is forbidden by
the Church."

After another round of delicious coffee options and more snacks, Teresa asked Michael for another nugget of his wisdom.

"Don't try to fit in; shine forth."

"Even in grade school we Tent-City kids had counselors working with us. Later, I realized that probably the government wanted to get the next generation off the public assistance lists by normalizing us."

"We may not have known the term 'misfit,' but we certainly had the experience of not fitting in with the in-group in our classes. After all, since our parents didn't have cars, we never went to karate classes or little-league. I did like playing games in the gym or the school playground, but I was always chosen last for any team.

"It was in High School when I started getting all this positive attention for looking like Jesus that I first thought: maybe the purpose of life is not to fit in, but rather to shine forth."

"Oh, I love it," Teresa said as she wrote the gist of his words on her notepad.

A seminarian used the opportunity to say: "After all, Jesus didn't fit in with the Pharisees and the Saducees, but he sure shone forth."

Moving along - "I carry the weight of every person on my back." He paused, then explained: "I guess that sense came out of dragging people out of the deep water as a lifeguard. You could count on the legs of a centipede how many times parents sit under an umbrella napping or texting and don't notice that their children are way too far out in the sea for safety."

Paul Quinn jumped in, "I'm going to take that image back to

the seminary for what a priest should do for his parishioners, drag them on their backs out of dangerous waters!"

Teresa began to think that in her article she certainly shouldn't label Michael as a New Age cult leader since he would surely read the article, but…maybe, instead a New Age sage.

Teresa pointed to this nugget for Michael to comment on next: "Nature is God – the ocean is God as ocean. The tree is God as tree, and so on. I am God as Michael."

"This insight came to me one day at twilight when the sun beams were sparkling on the waves at the ocean. Forgive me if I sound disrespectful, but the way some religious people talk about God you would think God was just a word to be used as a curse or as a blessing but nothing as magnificent as an ocean."

The seminarian, Steve, replied, "That's okay. We want to hear what you think. You're right in part. The admonition not to take the Lord's name in vain surely includes the use of the word God in

'God damn,' said so often by some people, even seminarians when startled by something that makes us angry…just the same, we think that God is the Creator of the ocean and the trees and of us…far greater, infinitely greater, so we would see thinking of Steve as God to be a way of belittling God."

Teresa looked down at the list on the page: "When you want to make a fist, open your hand, and bless the other person."

And more: "No hate, no fear, everyone is welcome here (a sign on my cabin door.)"

Then, quotes from others, mostly learned from seminarian friends:

"Love is a response to the unique preciousness of the other person." (Von Hildebrand)

"Leisure is the basis of culture." (Pieper)

"You can only love yourself loving." (Aquinas)

"Beauty is truth, truth beauty, that is all you need to know on earth." (Keats)

"Friendship: are you real, or did I invent you in my loneliness. I

touch the rough edges and rest se-
cure." (Anonymous)

Feeling a little tired, Teresa
suggested they postpone the other
nuggets on Michael's list for another session. She asked Paul to
work up some general religious
topics for dialogue among the
seminarians to which he readily
agreed.

Paul walked Teresa out to her
car: "I'll work the questions up and
give them out to the seminarians
first and e-mail them to you...also
give them to Michael?"

"No. Don't give them to our pseudo-Messiah. Let's see how he fields them spontaneously."

Back in his room at St. Mark's, Paul had a hard time getting to sleep. What Michael said about women triggered memories of Angela, the woman he had loved the most of the girlfriends he had in High School and in the Community College.

"Angela certainly wasn't boring!"

Brought up in a strict Catholic family, he was told never to have sex with any girl until he was married. But kissing wasn't a sin. And mild petting was marginal, with some priests telling them it was wrong, and others thinking that if the couple loved each other, it was okay. And then, there was always masturbation, with some priests insisting that if done not half in sleep but consciously, it was always a sin and others being more flexible. It was only when porn became a hugely diagnosed addiction that Paul became convinced that masturbation, consciously performed, was always wrong. This was after a talk at the seminary by

Matt Fradd, a converted porn addict.

Paul met Angela at a classical music concert at the Community College he went to for two years before entering the seminary. He was immediately attracted to this woman soloist who seemed to combine spiritual beauty in her eyes with a curvy body.

After the concert, Paul approached Angela and asked if he could escort her to the after-concert buffet. At that time, Paul was thinking he might have a vocation to become a priest, but he was not sure. The vocation director of the Archdiocese of Los Angeles had told him it could be good for him to attend a community college for two years before deciding. "Dating some young women could give you a better idea if could consider the rule of celibacy."

Later, once at the seminary, he learned that some administrators blamed the sex-scandals of the clergy as partly due to candidates entering the junior seminary for High School before their sexual energies had fully developed.

Paul dated a few women in his freshman year, but it was only Angela with whom he fell in love. Especially, they shared a love for music and for literature. Typical dates involved going to a concert and then talking for hours about books they read, often taking out two copies of the same book from the campus library. Tolstoy's *War and Peace* was their favorite.

Though Angela was not religious and didn't think pre-marital sex was wrong, she agreed to keep their physical relationship to a minimum for Paul's sake. His confessions would almost always include masturbation after sexual touching with Angela.

Paul's efforts to stop masturbating were amplified after reading an explanation in a book of C.S. Lewis, one of his all-time favorite novelists. Lewis was refuting the idea that if God created men with so much lust, masturbation was natural. Lewis thought that God allowed that strong desire for sex in males so that they would become husbands and fathers in order to satisfy it. That motive would lead them into a good family lifestyle whereas sex before marriage was just prolonging their selfish desires for a life of pleasure without obligation.

The decision to break up with Angela came to Paul during a vocation's retreat at St. Peter's Seminary. During one of the quiet prayer sessions, Paul was mesmerized by the expression on the face of the famous painting of Jesus by Agemian on the cover of a book:

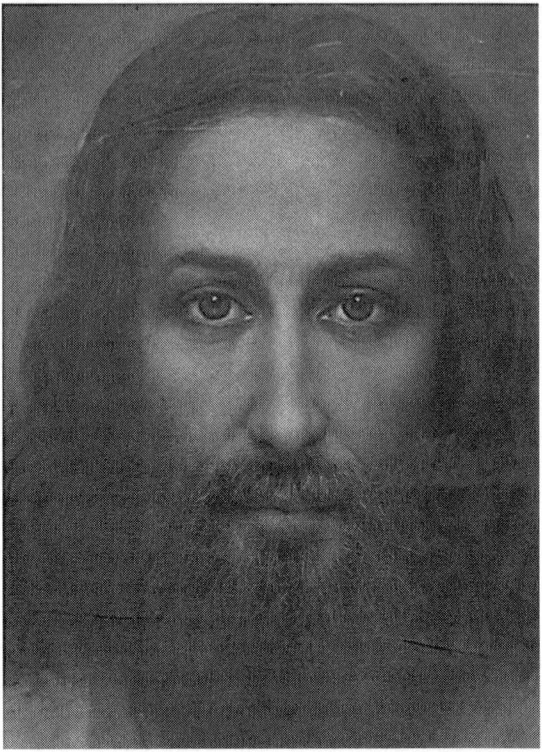

On their next date after that re-treat, over their usual cappuccinos, Paul grabbed her arm.

"My dear, dear, Angela, love of my life, I have news glad and bad."

Somehow, Angela knew right away from the tone of his voice that it would be something glad for him and bad for her.

"See this picture. He showed her the Agemian Jesus on the cover of that book he borrowed from the retreat center."

"That's beautiful, Paul. I don't remember ever seeing it."

"I'd like you to read this book. It's about all the reasons Christians believe that Jesus is our Savior. I'll need you to return it, though." He handed her the book.

Tears came into his dark blue eyes. "I have often told you that you are the most wonderful young woman I have ever met and that I hoped one day we would become man and wife."

"That's my hope also, Paul dear."

"But it's not going to happen. At least I don't think so. During my retreat, through the eyes of that very picture of Jesus, I felt Him calling me to become His priest."

After a few minutes of silence, Angela said softly: "Paul, I am not surprised. All along, I have had the feeling that, in spite of your love for me, it wouldn't work out…Just know that unless I am with some-one else, if you ever decide the priesthood isn't for you, after all, I will still want you for myself."

4

When Teresa arrived home at
11 PM, her husband woke up long
enough to ask her how the interview went.

"Amazing, actually, John. This
character is somehow different
from anyone I ever met! He looks
so much like Jesus in *The Passion*.
Even though he's not a Christian,
when he looks at me, I feel as if it
were Jesus looking at me!"

The rest of the workday Teresa
spent on her usual weekly assignment – special events at each of the

many churches in the Archdiocese culled from their parish bulletins.

Happily, the efficient seminarian Paul Quinn e-mailed her the dialogue questions he had come up with. These would be central to the article she would write for *The Catholic Weekly* about how Catholics can dialogue with New Agers.

Questions for Dialogue:

(After Michael talks, each one of you seminarians be prepared to either respond to what he said or tell the rest what you think the best answer is.)

What do you think the meaning of life is?

What is your favorite adjective for what God is like?

Who are your favorite heroes or heroines?

What actions are bad?

Is there life after death?

Can people be good by themselves, or do they need to go often to a religious meeting?

Teresa liked the way the questions were framed. Exactly. Part of dialogue mode is not to talk about things in one's own lingo but that of the interlocutor. So, not 'Why aren't you a Catholic?' But 'Do you think people need to go to religious meetings?'

The following Thursday evening found Teresa back at the Metro café. Michael was wearing the same plaid woolen shirt with threads hanging out of the seams. The seminarians were, once again, dressed in perfect white button-down shirts and black pants.

She had decided for a change to look more feminine, even a bit hippie-like, wearing a striped flowing cotton ankle length dress. The last minute in the car she undid the rubbery yellow ribbon that tied her brown hair up in a bun and let her tresses flow below her shoulders. "Vanity, thy name is woman," she quoted Shakespeare laughing at herself. "I guess I don't like looking so old and motherly to these twenty and thirty-year-olds."

And, this time, Michael didn't reach across the table to greet her by taking her hand, but, instead, he walked around the table and gave her a hug.

Teresa considered her marriage to be happy in spite of the usual personality conflicts of one sort or another couples have to deal with, so she was surprised that night when she had a dream that her husband John died, and she entered into an affair with this twenty-years younger Michael!

Bringing analysis of the dream to her daily personal prayer time, she recalled an article she read about consecrated widows. This vocation of the early Church was being revived. "Jesus, if you choose to take John first, call me to be your consecrated bride… and, meanwhile, keep me from crazy fantasies of second husbands."

Back at the Café Metro, Teresa sipped a few more mouthfuls of her cappuccino and started the dialogue:

"Michael, if you recall, I asked Paul Quinn to work up a list of questions for tonight."

"Paul, will you read the questions?"

"Tell us, Michael, what do you think the meaning of life is?"

"To become what you are!" replied Michael, dark brown eyes blazing with energy.

One of the seminarians nodded and asked: "Michael, we believe that after original sin we are a mixture of good and evil, so becoming what we are isn't such a good idea. We want to become better through God's grace."

Michael thought for a few minutes. "I wouldn't put it that way, but I see what you mean. 'To become what you are,' means to me to become that best self that is often lying dormant under all sorts of bad habits."

Another seminarian entered the dialogue, now trialogue? "I was addicted to drugs before my conversion. That self I was when taking drugs was kind of blissful for a while…but then led to dropping out of Church. I even lived on the street for a while. Even though I felt relatively happy, I wasn't doing anything to help anyone else, except to connect them to pushers!"

Teresa and the seminarians laughed as he emphasized his joke.

Michael reached across the table, though, for the hand of that ex-drug addict. "I know what you're saying. I was into that for a short time, but then I decided that

I didn't want to be dependent on a substance to be happy."

Paul went on to the second question: "Michael, what is your favorite adjective for what God is like?"

Michael's dark brown eyes shone with joy. "That's easy! God is all."

A seminarian, sarcastically retorted: "Oh, you mean God is a mosquito and God is S.H.I.T?"

Paul broke in. "Okay, Fred, since we are practicing dialogue techniques, why don't you think of a way to frame that question that is more appealing."

Fred thought a little while. It wouldn't be good if Paul told the rector about his using the 'S-word.'

"I'll give it a try."

"Michael, I can see why you would think that God is the ocean or the sun, as you like to say, but what about yucky things like mosquitos or defecation?"

Suddenly, a siren blared from the street. The flaring red color of the lights of a police vehicle could be seen from the large picture windows of the Metro Café.

Michael dashed out the door followed by Paul.

A seminarian led the group at the table in prayer: "Lord, Jesus, help whoever is in peril. Bring aid through the hands of the first responders. Hail Mary, full of grace…pray for us sinners, now and at the hour of our death."

Twenty minutes later, the siren blared again as the police car departed.

Michael and Paul returned.

"Amazing!" exclaimed Michael. "When we got to the beach, the policeman was just about to call for the ambulance. The man lying in the arms of our night-watchman looked like a Tent-City type. Paul laid a crucifix on the chest of the man. He immediately jumped up. He glanced at everyone in bewilderment and said, 'Guess I shouldn't try to swim in the ocean after so much booze!' The police made him walk around to see if he was okay. One of them came over to us. He knew me from many such police calls. He said to Paul: 'I'm a Catholic, so I know what you were doing. God bless you. Maybe I got to see a miracle?'

Paul then replied, 'It's good in any case. I'm a seminarian at St. Peter's up the highway. Come visit us sometime.'"

Teresa called John to say she'd be late. She also begged the manager to keep the Café open another half hour later than usual so she could finish the interview.

"How about a second round of coffee and munchies on *The Catholic Weekly*?" Teresa offered.

When the tall bejeweled barista finished distributing the order, Teresa reached over to Paul. "Would you mind taking off that crucifix and letting me hold it while we talk?"

Larger than the decorative 1 1/2" crucifix that some Catholics wear, Paul's was almost three inches long. Looking around, Teresa saw that all the seminarians wore an identical crucifix.

"Michael, you must have seen near drownings often at the beach. Would you say this was a miracle?"

"To tell you the truth, I like to say that everything is a miracle."

"Paul, why don't you explain the Catholic concept of a miracle?"

Paul nodded and replied, "The issue of whether a cure is a miracle or not comes up especially regarding canonization procedures."

Michael leaned in toward Paul, listening carefully.

Paul continued, "It would not be good for Christians to think that every unexpected healing is a miracle. Why not? Well, some such seeming healers could set themselves up as leaders and then lead their followers astray."

Michael asked, "So, what then do you teach is a real miracle?"

"It has to be instantaneous. There has to be no natural explanation for it…So, obviously, the man who seemed to have drowned at the beach tonight could have simply passed out from drinking too much and then revived."

"Right, Paul," the seminarian, Steve, joked. "If I decided tonight that you were a miracle-worker just because this man didn't die from drowning, I would have to obey you day and night at the seminary!"

Everyone but Michael laughed.

5

On the long drive home, Teresa pondered the miracle or non-miracle that had interrupted the dialogue about the questions Paul had cooked up.

What effect might that experience tonight on the beach have on "the Messiah of the Metro Café," as she had started calling him in her mind.

"Oh, dear Jesus, I pray, may this sincere seeker, Michael, find You so much more wonderful than his 'divine within' concepts."

She could have written her article on Dialoguing with New Agers without another interview, but she decided that getting his responses to the other questions Paul had listed would enrich the article.

So, on the following Thursday she was back again at the Café Metro. Even in Southern California it gets a little colder in December, leading Teresa to wear a red sweater over her blue pants. To match Michael's red plaid shirt?

After putting in their usual coffee and goodies order, Paul began the next dialogue question.

"Who are your favorite heroes or heroines, Michael?"

"As a kid I had the usual ones, Spiderman, for instance...but then in High School I became fascinated with the Buddha. I also loved reading about Solzhenitsyn's Harvard Address when he shocked all of us Americans by saying that escaping from the evils of Communist Russia to come the U.S., he was appalled by the evils of consumerism. When I explored my Jewish heritage a little, of course, I did admire Moses and Isaiah."

"What about heroines?" a seminarian asked.

Michael took a few minutes. "I liked re-runs of Katherine Hepburn movies…she was so different from the brainless sexy actresses like Marilyn Monroe."

"As you would expect, Michael," a seminarian joined in, "our greatest hero is Jesus and our greatest heroine is Mary. If you never read the New Testament, maybe you would like to try, setting aside all prejudices you might have."

"Certainly."

The seminarian handed Michael a New Testament.

Teresa took down all these answers in shorthand on her notepad.

"Now, Michael, this one might be a toughie for dialogue with us, but what actions do you think are bad?"

"Violent ones, and of any kind. Wars, naturally, but also capital punishment, gang murders. I never watch Westerns since they take shooting people almost for granted."

Steve signaled he wanted to provide a different point of view. "Michael, you don't mean that on your beach watch if someone started holding someone up with a gun you wouldn't try to stop him to protect an innocent person, do you?"

"That would be part of my job. But the few times I needed to use force during a fight, I always used the least necessary. I will push the aggressor to the ground and sit on him rather than punch him out."

Paul then challenged Michael about abortion as violence.

"Even as a teenager living in Tent-City and going to the public school I always rejected abortion. I can still remember the first time my parents mentioned it and explained what it was. 'But, isn't a baby the most innocent possible victim?' I insisted."

"Do you think there is life after death, Michael?"

"I sure hope so! Actually, often when I hear of a death or witness the death of someone who has drowned, I have visions of the spirit of that person leaving their bodies and floating above us."

The Filipino seminarian told them that just such a vision of his father's soul after his death was part of his decision to become a priest. "When the priest came to anoint my father, my Dad stopped groaning and a beatific smile came on his face. 'Jesus, Jesus, Jesus,' he called out and then, 'Jesus, take me.' With that he stopped breathing."

Delighted with the progress of the dialogue, Teresa couldn't wait to see what Michael would say about the last question.

"Can people be good by themselves, or do they need to go to a religious meeting, Michael?"

"Michael smiled. Since all of you are Catholics who go to services, it's a no-brainer that we will not agree on this one. From time to time, I go to someone's funeral in a Church or in a Jewish service. They always seem to me to be kind of stiff and formal. If I were in charge, I would make up a spontaneous prayer related to the personality of the one who had died."

Not sure if she could finagle from *The Catholic Weekly* still another Thursday session, Teresa decided to use the last hour of this one for sharings.

"How about each of you tell Michael why you love the Catholic Church so much?"

Here are some of the responses she jotted down:

"I went to a public High School but went every week to a youth group in the Church. They let me play the trumpet for our praise and worship. Something about the joy in that music changed me from thinking of the Church as an empty ritual to loving Jesus and realizing He sent the Holy Spirit to devise a way that He could reach us throughout the centuries."

"In public school, we learned about how the French revolutionaries hated the Church. They taught the poor to reject the priests – 'they live in that rich Church paid for by the donations of you poor.' But in Los Angeles, where I lived near the Cathedral, I saw Catholics going in and out all day long, not just for Sunday Mass. I began to think of the Church building as my celestial living room and of the priests, not as exploiters, but kind of as our slaves."

Lots of laughter followed that one.

"I found Sunday Mass very boring when I was a child. When my favorite grandmother died I was only ten years old. Listening to the words of the funeral Mass, I suddenly realized that if I hoped to ever see grandma again it would depend on those words being true...that Jesus died to prepare a home for us in heaven."

"Michael, next Thursday is Thanksgiving. Most of us leave

Wednesday to visit our families until Sunday night, but mine are off on a trip to Arizona to be with my sister's family. Maybe I could pick you up and bring you to see our beautiful seminary."

"Thanks, Paul, but you would not believe how busy we are at the beach during holidays. People driving all the way from Santa Barbara to L.A. or the opposite trip from Orange County all the way up to San Francisco stop at the Café Metro for a coffee break and then walk over to the ocean-side. I have to make sure no wandering children decide on a swim and get into trouble."

"I get it…well, if you decide to take a break, here is my phone number. Give me a ring."

Before leaving the café, Teresa announced: "Friends, this may be my last time interviewing Michael for my article…Here is my card. I'm going to send you a draft of my article. Please text me immediately with any corrections or suggestions."

"How about a closing prayer?" Paul corralled them. Holding hands in a circle around the table he began: "Thank you, God, for creating each one of us. Thank you for our fruitful fellowship. Keep us safe. Holy Spirit enlighten Teresa as she tries to convey the wisdom shared at this table with the wider Church."

"Thank you for Michael, our friend," Teresa added simply.

The next day after picking up the night litter on the beach, Michael opened up the New Testament the seminarian had given him.

What struck him most was how counter-cultural Jesus was. One would think that he would have been like the zealots protesting the Roman conquerors, or like the Pharisees, helping ordinary Jews to keep the law in spite of challenges. But, no, there he was proclaiming a way of life seemingly impossible for anyone who wanted to survive – turning the other cheek, forgiving 70x7 times, loving one's enemies, never calling anyone even a fool!

Michael knew that conventionally religious people dubbed thinkers like himself, who weren't members of any specific group, as New-

Agers. He did identify with some ways New-Agers thought of reality but not all. Openness to truth under any name seemed to him to be a necessity. That was part of why he liked to dialogue with the seminarians. And, after reading the New Testament in its entirety, he could see that knowing the figure of Jesus more personally could be helpful for his own growth.

On Thanksgiving evening, the café manager brought a cell-phone over to Michael at his usual table.

"Michael, dear, this is Teresa Domingo, the reporter working on the story. It happens I have time tomorrow morning since my office is closed for the weekend. Could I come to see you at the beach around 10 AM to show you the draft of my article? I want to be sure nothing in it will make you think anything personal you said was a violation of our collaboration."

"Sure. Just park at the Metro Café and walk across the highway to the beach. You will see me on top of the life-guard tower. Here's my cell phone number just in case I am not right there for any reason…of course, if duty calls we will have to interrupt our chat."

As usual, traffic on the Pacific Coast Highway on the Friday of Thanksgiving was minimal. It took Teresa only half the time it usually did on Thursday evenings. Sure enough, Michael was in a bathing suit on the platform of the life-guard tower. The beach was almost empty.

Michael climbed down and of-fered her a canvas chair next to a fold up table on the beach.

Teresa handed him a print-out of the article to vet. It started with an introduction about the need for dialogue among people of different beliefs and how her interviews with the group of seminarians around a man who seemed like a New-Age sage had proceeded.

Michael smiled at the description of himself as looking just like Jesus and the seminarians in their proscribed uniform white and black uniforms. He checked out the part about his background. No problems.

Just then a group of children approached the table. There were two boys around nine and ten years old and an adorable little girl of about five years old. Michael introduced Teresa as an important newspaper reporter and told them to enjoy themselves until he called them back later for their usual presents.

"Wait! Where are your parents?"

"They went to the Metro," one of the boys said. "They told us to be sure to watch Tricksy."

He found it particularly interesting to read Teresa's list of principles for dialogue with New Agers:

- Listen to the person first – don't just lecture.
- Never assume they have no wisdom even if it is only a half-truth from the Catholic point of view.
- Always share your own experience–people are more attracted to stories than to logical proofs.
- Become friends so you don't remind them of teachers they disliked.

"Right on, Teresa! Did you ever teach the seminarians before they met me?"

"No. I culled this from watching what went well and not so well during the sessions."

He saw brief paragraphs about his nuggets of wisdom ending with a question mark. "What is that for?"

"Oh, yes, Michael, one of them on that list that I didn't understand was Thomas Aquinas' 'you can only love yourself loving.' Can you explain it more?"

"The seminarians taught me that from their class in philosophy of love. It's like this. When you are not being loving, but instead you are angry or disgusted or bitter, you can't love yourself. Check it out – look in the mirror when you are feeling unloving. You look awful. But when you are delighting in people or serving them you feel and look lovable."

There was a paragraph about how Michael did deep breathing prayers and how the seminarians related that to their Catholic way of doing centering prayer – sitting quietly with hands unfolded and eyes closed and breathing in an out the name of Jesus or Mary or God the Father, or the Holy Spirit.

At this point a tourist bus stopped at the beach parking lot. Michael excused himself to see what they wanted. "Probably won't take too long, Teresa. Usually they stop here after getting coffee and snacks at the Metro to use our many porta-potties and admire the ocean."

Teresa looked over the rest of the article. She noticed from a distance that the two little boys she met earlier were running up to the people on the bus.

When the bus took off Michael walked back to the table with the boys. Michael whispered in Teresa's ear "They're from the Tent-City. When they see regular people, they like to beg for coins."

"Where's your sister, guys?"

They looked at the shoreline. No one in sight.

"Weren't you supposed to watch her?"

"Well, she was digging this big hole..."

Michael ran toward the ocean and still seeing no Tricksy dove into the water.

Teresa prayed, "Dear God. I should have noticed what they

were doing when Michael left for the bus people. Please let that sweet little girl be okay."

Not okay. Michael emerged with the little girl's body on his back. He threw her down on the sand and started CPR.

Later, he told Teresa he had prayed this way: "If I am God as Michael or even a twenty-first century Messiah, let my hands heal this dear little child."

After ten minutes he yelled to Teresa to call 911.

6

Years later, when Fr. Michael Kaufman was telling Catholics about his conversion, he would always say: "The death of little Tricksy was the turning point. I couldn't save her, but, I believe, Jesus on Paul's crucifix did save that drowned man. I didn't create her, but God the Father did…I realized finally that I was not the savior but Jesus might be my Savior."

Then he would recount at conference talks, on Catholic radio, and on TV and webinars, the rest of the story:

"After the funeral of Tricksy, I asked Paul to come and bring me to the seminary. In his room, I saw the Agemian painting of Jesus. When I looked into His merciful eyes, I felt his personal love for me flowing out of them. Next came watching the old movie *Jesus of Nazareth* and then *The Passion*.

"From seeing what crucifixion really was in that so graphic movie of Mel Gibson and, also, in a certain way, identifying with Jim Caviezel's Jesus because I, Michael, looked so much like him, the take-away was Paul's understanding:

"'Some Catholics object to the violence in that movie. But I think it is the proof of the resurrection. How would those frightened apostles and disciples ever risk such a crucifixion of themselves by identifying themselves as followers of Jesus, unless they had seen the resurrected Jesus and touched Him?'"

Michael would continue, "This led me first to become a Messianic Jew – that is a Jew who believes Jesus was the promised Messiah, but doesn't join a Christian Church.

"Later, I found the Association of Hebrew-Catholics where the practice of the Catholic faith includes Jewish holidays and some customs so that Jews who become Catholics don't feel they have lost their Jewish identity.

"That was followed by attending some Masses at the seminary with my old friends from the Metro Café.

"After that came a sense that maybe I, myself, was called to become a baptized Catholic and maybe, even, a priest.

"Although a rector will usually not allow seminarians to wear long, long hair and long beards because they could look like drug addicts, in my case they decided to make an exception. The rector told me, 'We think that even as a seminarian you could attract non-believers if you look like Jesus.'"

And, in fact, during his years at the seminary, Michael was sent on Thursday evenings to the Metro Café as a witness. A tradition he continues to this day.

Made in the USA
Columbia, SC
06 January 2023

75728293R00061